Charlotte Zolotow
I Know a Lady
pictures by
James Stevenson

Greenwillow Books, New York

On our block
there is a lady
who lives alone.

She works in her garden
and gives us daffodils in the spring,
zinnias in the summer,

chrysanthemums in the fall,
and red holly berries
when the snow falls.

She waves to us
mornings on our way to school
and smiles when we pass her house
coming home.

She invites us in to warm up
at her fire at Halloween
and gives us candy apples
she's made herself.

And at Christmas she asks us in
to see her tree
and gives us cookies
sprinkled with red and green dots.

At Easter she makes little cakes
with yellow frosting.

Sometimes we see her walking
alone
along the path in the woods
behind the houses.
She smiles at me
and knows my name is Sally.
She pats my dog
and knows her name is Matilda.

She feeds the birds
and puts cream out for the old cat
who lives across the meadow.

I wonder what she was like
when she was a little girl.
I wonder if some old lady
she knew
had a garden and cooked and smiled
and patted dogs
and fed the cats
and knew her name.

If I was an old lady
and she was a little girl
I would love her a lot
the way I do now.